Sarah Whitcher's Story

Sarah Whitcher's Story

Elizabeth Yates
illustrated by Nora S. Unwin

Bob Jones University Press, Greenville, South Carolina 29614

Library of Congress Cataloging-in-Publication Data

Yates, Elizabeth, 1905-
    Sarah Whitcher's Story / by Elizabeth Yates : illustrated by Nora S.
Unwin.
        p.   cm.
    Summary: Describes the search for and adventures of a young girl
lost in a New Hampshire forest in the pioneer days. Based on a true
incident.
    ISBN 0-89084-754-1
    [1. Frontier and pioneer life—New Hampshire—Fiction.
2. Survival—Fiction. 3. New Hampshire—Fiction.] I. Unwin, Nora
Spicer, 1907-   ill. II. title.
PZ7.Y213Sar   1994
[Fic]—dc20   94-
27185

                                                           CIP
                                                           AC

Sarah Whitcher's Story
Elizabeth Yates
Cover by John Roberts
Illustrations by Nora S. Unwin

© 1994 Bob Jones University Press
Greenville, South Carolina 29614

Printed in the United States of America

ISBN 0-89084-754-1

15   14   13   12

Contents

Books for Young People by Elizabeth Yates

Amos Fortune, Free Man
Carolina's Courage
The Journeyman
Hue & Cry
Sound Friendships
The Next Fine Day
Mountain Born
A Place for Peter
Sarah Whitcher's Story

Chapter One
Sunup to Sundown

"Sarah!" Pa's voice was as sharp and clear as the sound of his ax when it bit into a tree. And it meant one thing.

Putting down the wood chips with which she was playing, Sarah trotted toward the cabin. Ollie, the big black dog, loped along beside her.

Pa stood in the doorway, the dinner horn in his hand. The other children had quickly responded to the sound of the horn, but it always seemed to take Pa's voice to get Sarah.

She ran to him. With one swift move, he scooped her up in his arms, and she rode on his shoulder the rest of the way.

"What were you doing?"

"Building a cabin, like the kind you built for us."

"Didn't Ollie tell you it was time for the noonday meal?"

"Ollie was asleep."

They went into the cabin and Pa set Sarah down on the bench by the trestle table where the rest of the family was gathered.

"Seems we always have to wait for Sarah," eleven-year-old Reuben grumbled.

Joseph, younger by a year and quick to copy Reuben in everything, frowned at his sister. Little John, eight years old and hungry, drummed his spoon on the table.

"Children," Ma said gently, "that's no way to act on the Sabbath." Her hand, just touching the cradle near one end of the table, continued to rock Baby Henry.

"But we're hungry, Ma," wailed five-year-old Betsey.

Ollie squeezed himself under the table to lick one bare foot after another of the several swinging there, then he settled himself for sleep.

As soon as Pa sat down, heads bowed and hands stilled as each one waited for him to speak the blessing.

"We're thankful, Lord, for all the good things you've given us, and we'll eat this food to grow strong in your service. Amen."

The "Amen" in which everyone joined was all but lost in the sound of wooden spoons against wooden bowls.

Sunday was different from other days in more ways than its food, not only in the Whitcher cabin near the crest of Pine Hill, but in every home that made up the settlement of Warren. Work was set aside in forest, field, and household.

Joseph interrupted his eating to ask, "Why do we say thanks for this food? We said thanks for it yesterday when it was hot; now it's cold."

Pa's answer was brief and not to be questioned further, as his words came from the Bible. *"In everything give thanks."*

Most of the hundred or so people of the township lived in cabins in clearings on the mountain slopes. Only a few lived in the valley through which the Baker River ran. There, at the crossing of wagon tracks and bridle trails, was a gristmill where the settlers brought their wheat to be ground and a sawmill for their logs. But there was no place for

Sunday worship. Until a meetinghouse was built, each family kept the Sabbath in its own way. Horses might neigh, cattle low, sheep bleat, hens cackle, but no sound of work would be heard.

Reuben had asked his father why this was so, and the answer had been as certain as all Pa's answers. "It's a rule of life. Six days we work from sunup to sundown; on the seventh we rest."

"But not from sunup to sundown."

"Not quite," his father had agreed, smiling at Reuben.

There were always some necessary chores that had to be done, even on Sunday. Everyone helped with them, and since they were few, a good part of the day remained for each one to spend as he liked. That part began for the Whitchers after the noon meal when Pa read aloud from the Bible.

Wooden bowls were soon emptied, noggins of milk were drained, and all put into a basket to be taken later to the brook for washing. Then the family drew up in a loose circle by the slumbering ashes on the hearth. There was no need for a fire, but this was always the chosen place for reading and listening. Warm as the June weather was, ashes would never be allowed to get completely cold, since fire was part of the life in a settler's cabin.

Ma picked up Baby Henry and nestled him in her arms. Betsey sat near, leaning against Ma's skirts. Joseph and Reuben sat back to back. Little John took his favorite place near the chimney. Hands that on other days might have busied themselves with carding or whittling were folded in laps or sunk deep in pockets. Sarah lay on the floor beside Ollie. Snuggling against him, she let her fingers move in and out of his shaggy hair.

"What you going to read to us, Pa?" Joseph asked as he watched his father take the big Bible down from its shelf.

"We've reached the book of Job, and that's where we'll begin today."

Pa read the first two chapters. Job was a good man and Pa understood him. He had a fine wife and family, land and stock, but the story didn't really begin until Satan told God that Job wouldn't be such a good man if the Lord hadn't been so kind to him. God gave Satan a chance to test Job, and one calamity after another happened. Soon Job had nothing left. Satan wanted to have another chance at testing Job's goodness and trust in the Lord. God told Satan to do what he liked but to spare Job's life.

"Job must have been a sight." Pa looked up from the page. "Poor now, without a home, covered with boils; and he must have felt mean. Even his wife told him to give up." Pa looked down at the page and read again. *"What? Shall we receive good at the hand of God, and shall we not receive evil?* That was what Job said to his wife."

"Did he die, Pa?" Reuben asked.

"He did not. What kind of a story would that be?" Pa's hands were turning the pages quickly. The children liked it when he skipped to get on with the story.

"Three of his friends came to see him, and then a fourth," Pa went on. "They talked and talked because they thought Job had brought his troubles on himself. Job had plenty to say, too, but he never said anything against the Lord."

"What happened?"

"Listen. Here's the best part of the book. It begins at the thirty-eighth chapter and it goes right on to the end. *Then the Lord answered Job out of the whirlwind—*" Pa read with as much gusto as if the Lord had been speaking directly to him.

Sarah stopped playing with Ollie's hair to watch her father. The three boys stared at their father. Ma looked across the baby's face and the top of Betsey's head to rest her eyes on her husband, watching as well as listening.

"Then Job answered the Lord, and said, I know that thou canst do everything." There were only a few more verses and Pa read more slowly to make them last. *"The Lord gave Job twice as much as he had before . . . and blessed the latter end of Job more than his beginning."* When the story was over, Pa said, "It's sure enough that the Lord can do great things."

Ma sighed. "It's a wonderful story, John."

"But," Joseph said, looking intently at Pa, "what did Job *do?*"

"He trusted, son. No matter what happened, he knew the Lord would make everything come out right."

"And He did," Sarah said, though more to Ollie than to anyone else.

The closing of the book was the signal for dismissal, but Pa kept it open, so the children waited.

"Ma," he said. He looked at her over the boys' heads, each one with hair as red as his own. "Let us walk up to the Summit to see Chase and Hannah."

Pleased at the prospect, Ma nodded.

"We'll be back by sundown." Pa looked at Reuben. "So see that the stock is cared for and fed. Joseph, have an eye to the fire. See that the ashes don't get cold and that there is wood on the hearth for the night. Little John, you are to mind the ones younger than yourself—Betsey, Sarah, and the baby. Ollie will help."

"Yes, Pa," the boys chorused.

After the Bible was put away, Pa placed his big muscular hand on the head of one boy after another. It was not the first time he had given them such a charge. They accepted it, each one aware of his particular responsibility. Then they ran out of the cabin to follow their own pursuits.

"Betsey," Ma said turning her attention to her daughter. "See that the bowls and spoons are washed, take good care of Baby Henry, and watch that Sarah doesn't get into any trouble."

"Yes, Ma." Betsey received the baby from her mother's arms. Proudly and carefully, she carried him to the cradle.

Sarah stood by the hearth with one arm around Ollie. "Want to go with you," she pleaded.

"No, Sarah." Ma was firm. "You must stay with the others. Ollie will play with you if the boys are too busy, and we'll bring something nice home to you all." Ma reached for her wicker basket. She never went away without it, as there was always something to be found that would be good to eat or to use or to look at.

Pa picked Sarah up and held her high in the air. She was a redhead, too, but the only one in the family with his pale blue eyes. Sometimes, when he looked into them, he felt that he was seeing his own in a glass. The others had their mother's dark eyes, and Betsey had her mop of brown curls. He set Sarah down on the doorstep, seized Ma's arm in the joy of the day and her company, and they were off. They went briskly up to the ridge, never once looking back, then, they ran as the path dipped down to Berry Brook.

Ollie pushed himself against Sarah, their heads almost on a level as they stood together in the doorway. From the back of the cabin came the sound of the boys' voices. Ollie slathered his tongue over the face near his muzzle, then moved slowly away, swinging his tail as he brushed by Sarah and went around the cabin to join the boys.

Sarah, moving as quietly as Ollie and keeping close to the cabin wall, followed him. When she reached the corner, she peeked around it to see what the boys were doing. Absorbed in their work, they were attaching disks of wood that Pa had planed for them to some boards they had nailed together to make a cart.

"As soon as we get this done," Reuben was saying, "we'll make Ollie pull it."

Little John was fashioning a harness from some scraps of leather. "Ollie," he called, "come here to me so I can see if this fits you."

Sarah decided there was no game here in which she could play, so she backed away from the cabin corner to see what Betsey might be doing.

Standing in the doorway and watching her sister, she soon realized that Betsey was far too occupied to be interested in a game. Baby Henry's sobs had become screams, demanding her attention, and Betsey's hands were full with him and his needs.

"You're wet, Henry, as wet as if you'd sat in Berry Brook, but you'll have to stay as you are until I find something dry for you." Betsey crossed the room to Ma's big chest to find a change for Henry.

Everybody was busy. Everybody had something to do. Except Sarah.

She turned around and watched a bird hopping along the path in front of her. It stopped, scratched at the ground, then cocked its head at her. "Come along with me," it seemed to say as it took wing and flew into the nearby woods.

Sarah decided to pretend she was Pa when he first came to Pine Hill. He would have had an ax in his hand, but she could not have one. His ax was almost as long as she was tall and she had never lifted it, but she could find a pretend ax.

Hunting for a piece of wood, she followed the bird. As soon as she found a stick that was the right size and that fitted her hand nicely, she was no longer Sarah but Pa, and the story he had told so often began to come alive in her.

It was all a long time ago when Pa lived in Salisbury, Massachusetts, many miles to the south. He was a big man and he wanted mountains around him, so one day he told Miss Sarah Marston that he was off to the high country to find good land and build a tight cabin. Sarah stopped and addressed herself to a birch tree.

Pretending she was Pa, she spoke to it as if it were Ma. She stood very straight and shifted the ax to her left hand so she could hold out her right to the tree. She bowed and said to the tree in a deep bold voice, "You'll be willing to change the hills for the mountains, won't you, Miss Marston?"

A shiver of wind in the leaves might have served as an answer, but Sarah wanted to make her own. She put down the stick and went to stand with her back against the birch tree.

Now she was Ma. She ran her hands down her skirt to smooth it, as Ma would. Putting one leg behind the other, she dropped a curtsey and in a high polite voice said, "Yes, Mr. Whitcher, I'll exchange anything but you."

Sarah stepped away from the tree and picked up the stick. She was Pa again, ax in hand, marching off to the mountains, head high, free arm swinging. Before she had gone far she turned for one more sight of the birch tree. "I'll be back," she said in as deep a voice as she could manage.

A year had gone by before Pa returned to Salisbury. He brought Ma the news that he had cleared land and built a cabin in the settlement of Warren, where the mountains were big and the streams cold and six other families had their homes.

It made Sarah feel brave and strong as she thought of all that Pa had done on Pine Hill.

She stopped for a moment to get her bearings, as she had often known Pa to do when she was with him, then she marched on down the slope and waded into Berry Brook. The feel of the cold water was good, but she did not stand in it long, for she was Pa and there was work to do.

On the far side of the brook the trees grew so tall they seemed to touch the sky. She found her way

among them, skipping sometimes over the pine needles and patches of moss, running often since there was no underbrush to catch at her and hold her back. Now and then she stood still and tilted her head to look up to the sky, but the branches of the trees met high above her, and she could not see the sky through their thick green.

After a while she came to a clearing where wild grasses grew. There were flowers among them and Sarah decided to pick some to take home to Ma. While she was picking, she saw something growing low on the ground that was even better than flowers. Strawberries! Thick as stars in the sky, they spread over the ground, especially where the grass was thin. Sarah reached down to pick one. The taste was ripe and sweet. Putting down her bunch of flowers and the stick, she picked and ate strawberries until she was full. Then she thought to pick some for Ma.

She had nothing to put them in, so she tried to make a basket of grasses as she had often seen Ma do. But the grass was slippery. She could not make the stalks stay together; even the knots she tied wouldn't hold. Sarah picked up her bunch of flowers and looked for the stick, but she couldn't find it.

"I don't need it now," she said to herself. It had been an ax to cut down trees to make a clearing and build a cabin, but there were no trees here. Pa would like this sunny meadow for the stock. Ma would like it for its flowers and berries. Now she could not get home quickly enough to tell them both about it.

The sun, poised on the tip of a near mountain, dipped slowly from sight. Clouds that had been gathering in the West began to move over the sky, and there was meaning in their grayness. Oncoming night and threatening rain were always reasons to seek shelter. Sarah, aware of the difference since the sun had gone, started to run toward the big trees.

It was darker among them than it had been in the clearing. Sarah ran more quickly until she was out of breath. She stopped for a moment and realized that she had not gotten anywhere. The forest was still all around her with its tall trees and the wind sighing through them. She listened, but she could not hear the sound of Berry Brook that would tell her she was nearing home.

"Pa!" she called. Rain started to patter on the leaves high above her head.

Chapter Two
Where Is Sarah?

As dusk came to the cabin with rain fast following it, Joseph and Reuben piled logs on the fire. Little John set the tin lantern in the open doorway. Henry, deprived of his mother too long, began to whimper. Betsey did her best to comfort him.

Standing in the doorway just back of the lantern, the three boys peered into the night.

"Could be the rain came sooner up at the Summit," Reuben suggested as explanation for his parents' lateness.

"Could be the path beside the river is slippery," Joseph added.

"Could be—" Little John could think of no reason, so he threw his arms around Ollie and hugged him.

Then out of the night came the sound they were hungering to hear—Pa's mighty shout. The boys answered with a chorus of shouts and Ollie barked excitedly. Soon Pa and Ma could be seen coming from the darkness of the woods and into the track of light made by the lantern. Stepping quickly as they came down from the ridge, they hurried to approach the shelter of the cabin.

"Where is Sarah?" Reuben asked, when he saw that only two and not three people had come back home.

"We didn't take her with us. She wanted to come, but she was told to stay home."

"Sarah's not here—" Joseph began.

"Sarah hasn't been here all afternoon," Reuben added.

Silence fell over them all. Betsey started to cry. Ma set her basket of berries on the bench by the door and reached quickly to gather the baby in her arms lest Betsey drop him. Little John, remembering now that he had been given the charge of the younger children, held himself tight against the shame and fear that gripped him.

"Is Sarah lost?" Ma turned to Pa.

His face was stern and his lips were drawn tightly together. "If she's strayed, we'll soon find her." He addressed his wife as if no one else were present, and he said four words she would not forget: "Trust in the Lord."

The baby started to wail. Ma held him closer, patting him comfortingly. She looked up and over Henry's head to give her husband the wisp of a smile. All the years she had known him she had never doubted his word. She would not doubt it now.

Pa looked at the children, calling their names one by one and drawing their eyes to him.

"Reuben, get the dinner horn and blow it hard. One long blast, then count ten before you sound it again."

"Yes, Pa."

"Joseph, go to the Richardsons' and tell them we need help."

"Yes, Pa. And on down to the Patches'?"

Pa nodded. "Betsey, have a care for what Ma wants you to do. If we don't find Sarah soon, we'll be needing something to eat." He turned away and started out into the night, then drew back as a spate of wind-driven rain spattered against the cabin. "It's a warm rain," he said, "and gusty. It won't last long."

Little John tugged at his father's breeches, then buried his head against them. "Pa, tell me what I can do, please, Pa."

"Stay here, son." The big hand reached down to steady the heaving of thin shoulders. "I'm going out to look for Sarah."

Pa left with the lantern. Calling Sarah's name constantly, he searched both sides of Berry Brook, particularly the places where Sarah liked to play, and the deep pools below the waterfalls where she had often helped her mother with the washing.

Standing a few paces away from the cabin, Reuben blew the dinner horn with all his strength. He knew that the sound, echoing in a series of long circling halloos, could be heard at a great distance. Late as it was, and raining, those who heard would respond.

Joseph raced down the hill to the nearest cabin, shouting as he approached. "Sarah's lost—lost."

Samuel Richardson asked no questions. He bade his wife keep an eye on the children and walked out of his cabin and up the slope to the Whitchers.

Hearing the sound of the horn, Joseph Patch stepped from his cabin in time to greet Joseph Whitcher.

"Is it fire, boy?"

"No—" Joseph fought hard to get breath enough to speak. "It's—Sarah—she's—lost."

Joseph Patch turned to his wife with a few words, then followed the boy into the night.

Within an hour nine men had arrived to join the search. Some answered the urgent blasts of the dinner horn; others heard the news as it raced from cabin to cabin.

"We'll soon find her," they said to assure Ma and the children. "Those little legs couldn't go too far."

Calling to each other, calling to Sarah, some worked slowly over the area within a half mile of the Whitcher cabin. They looked under brush, in hollows, by stumps and fallen logs. They held their lanterns toward any shelter where a child might have curled up in sleep. Some went much farther.

While they were gone, Ma and the boys built up a fire in the open space outside the cabin; then she sent them all to bed. They protested, but Ma was firm.

Betsey asked if she could have the cradle beside her. "I don't want Baby Henry to get out of my sight."

Ma laughed, to cheer herself as much as the children. She hugged Betsey. "Henry can't walk a step, but he may need watching all the same."

Little John lingered. "Ma, I'll keep my eyes on everyone in the cabin."

"Get some sleep, too, Little John. There'll be work for us all tomorrow."

Ollie followed the children, and Ma heaped more wood on the fire.

Pa, returning from his search that had yielded nothing, met two of the men at Berry Brook.

"We've been as far as the big boulder," one said.

"She couldn't have got that far!"

"She just might," the other replied, "but that's a varmint's den. She wouldn't have stayed there long."

Pa tried to be cheerful. "She's sleeping some-where. Come and dry yourselves by the fire."

The nine men stood around the fire with Ma and Pa, telling where they had gone, blaming their disappointment at not finding Sarah on the dark, and vowing they would find her as soon as morning came.

"Yes," Pa agreed, "we'll do better hunting with daylight to aid us, and a turn in the weather." He tilted his head to catch the direction of the breeze. "Wind out of the North will soon clear the rain away."

One by one the men took up their lanterns to return to their homes. "We'll be back in the morning."

Ma said, "I'll sit by the fire, John. You'll need rest for tomorrow. Take it under cover."

"How about yourself?"

"I'll watch for Sarah."

Pa heaved two more logs on the fire, logs that would be good for several hours' burning, then he left her. Once inside the cabin he took a quilt from the chest and spread it on the floor by the hearth. Through the open door he could see his wife outlined by the fire and beyond her the dark boles of the trees. Somewhere in those woods, his daughter was sheltered.

Determinedly he closed his eyes. Ma was right; a man needed sleep if he was to do his work well the next day. But Pa had long ago trained himself to sleep lightly. Should a sound be heard, he could spring quickly into action.

The night had many sounds for Ma, and at each one she alerted. When there was a whispering at the edge of the wood, she ran quickly toward it, stumbling in the darkness once she had left the circle of light. "Sarah, Sarah," she called, as she held her arms out to embrace her child.

There was no reply, and Ma had to admit to herself that the sound was only that made by leaves in the wind.

Another time she strained her ears, for the rippling of Berry Brook was like little Sarah's laughter.

She wanted to plunge into the dark and find her way down to the brook, but she told herself that a child would scarcely be laughing at such an hour.

Glancing toward the cabin, she saw her husband stretched out in sleep by the warm ashes. After a while she crept into the cabin to see if the children were sleeping soundly. The three boys were in the trundle bed. Betsey, at one side of the big bed, had an arm resting on the rim of the cradle that held the baby. Somewhere Sarah was sleeping, too, Ma told herself, and by the time another night had come around she would be safe in the bed beside her sister. The thought cheered Ma and she returned to sit by the fire. Yearning for morning, she threw sticks on to brighten the blaze, thinking light would speak to light and so hasten the coming day.

At last the long silence was broken by a bird calling in the woods. Soon there was an answering call; then the forest came alive with song, chatter, rustlings. Light began to filter through the trees. Blackness gave way to grayness. Strange shapes became familiar. Sheep bleated for pasture, the cow lowed to be milked, hens cackled for feed.

"Reuben! Joseph! Little John!" Pa called.

Startled out of sleep, Reuben responded first. "Is Sarah home?"

Joseph and Little John sat up. "Is she here? Is Sarah here?"

Pa shook his head. "Not yet. Come along out and help me with the stock."

Ma drew a bucket of water from the well. Some she tipped into a basin on the bench by the cabin door; the rest she carried to the hearth to begin preparations for breakfast. Henry whimpered.

"Bring him to me," Ma said to Betsey. "He'll be hungry and wet. I'll care for him. Make yourself ready for the day."

Soon they had drawn up to the trestle table. Wooden bowls had wild strawberries in them which Ma had brought back from the Summit—even the wooden bowl at the empty place.

Pa gave thanks. "For what You've given us. For the care You're taking of Sarah. Amen."

Under the table Ollie moved among the feet, licking each one in turn.

"Did you get the berries at Uncle Chase's?" Joseph asked.

"Yes. The field in front of their cabin was red with them."

"Was that what made you so late getting home?"

"Yes," Ma said. "I picked longer than I should."

Before they had finished, Uncle Chase stood in the doorway. "Whatever help you need, I'm here to give it."

Pa motioned his brother to sit at the empty place and, while he ate, told him what had happened.

Word about the Whitchers' lost child had traveled all over the township of Warren. Every man who could leave his work wanted to join in the search. So sure was one farmer of finding Sarah within a short time that he left his oxen yoked in the field. Another hung his scythe over the limb of a tree, certain he would be handling it again soon and could finish his swale before dusk.

Confident and high-spirited, they tramped up the bridle path from Warren, up the slope of Pine Hill to the Whitcher cabin. Some carried axes, two had long-barreled guns, each wore a dinner horn for signaling. The day was bright and warm.

By the time Pa, accompanied by Joseph and Reuben, returned from their search of the nearby woodland, twenty men had arrived at the cabin. They were all men of Warren. Some came from Beech Hill in the southerly part of the township, others from Height-o-Land to the north; three came from Runaway Pond and two from Patchbreuckland. All were known by name as neighbors; the Whitchers greeted them as friends.

Before setting out, Pa made sure they were familiar with the signals. "Three short sharp blasts in quick succession will give the good news that Sarah has been found," he said, "but we'll blow a single blast at intervals to keep us all in touch."

The men nodded. They knew the signals well. Then they were off.

Ma, standing in the doorway of the cabin with the baby in her arms and the four children near, waved.

"They'll find her, won't they, Ma?" Little John begged.

"They'll find her. We'll all be sitting together around the hearth by nightfall, and your father will be telling us a story. But you three boys have work to do, so you'd best get started. Betsey, I'll need your help if I'm to have something for those men to eat when they return. They'll be hungry."

The boys went toward barn, pasture, or vegetable patch to do the work Pa would have done with their help and now they had to do without him. Before they had gone far, Ma cried after them, "When I call your names, you're to call back."

"Yes, Ma," they chorused. Each one realized as never before the importance of knowing where each other was.

Over the outside fire an iron cauldron had been slung, and in it a meal would soon be simmering. When Ma needed more wood, she called to Little John. "Finish that last row you're hoeing and then get me some wood for this fire."

"Yes, Ma, and I'll put it in the cart so Ollie can help."

When Little John finished his row, he whistled to Ollie. Between the two of them, wood for a day's burning was brought and stacked within easy reach for Ma to put on the fire.

Led by Pa and Uncle Chase, the twenty men formed into two groups and fanned out into the woods, calling Sarah's name and signaling to each other at agreed intervals. Pa took his group down through the maple stand to Black Brook and Kelly Pond. Every imaginable place was searched, but not so much as a single clue—footprint or tatter of clothing—was discovered.

The group took counsel together and reluctantly agreed that this was not where Sarah had wandered. Willingly they followed their leader up the long climb past Oak Falls to Wachipauka Pond under the Webster Slide. Resting by the shore of the pond, they blew long, slow blasts as they called to the other searchers and to the little girl. The mountain wall gave back a sobbing echo.

"Where now, John?"

"Back to the cabin, searching as we go."

The descent was slow and difficult, giving them plenty of time to study the wilderness of rocks around them before they gained the cooling shade of the forest.

Uncle Chase took his group up the course of the Oliverian River. As they stopped to drink from one of its many pools, where the clear water revealed the shapes and colors of the stones over which it ran, more than one man had the same thought. A child stopping to drink or play, and losing balance, would soon be swept downstream by the force of the current. So they looked where the water swirled and turned in its course, but no one reported any kind of trace. They followed the river through a deep part of the forest to the foot of Moose Hillock on the far easterly side of the township.

Uncle Chase knew every tree, every boulder; even the darkest passes on the side of the mountain were familiar to him. Ten years ago he had been the first white settler to climb to the peak in pursuit of game, and soon after he had built his home in a lap of the mountain that commanded a wide sweep of the valley.

"No child could ever go this far," a man said, shaking his head wearily.

"I've been a hunter as long as I've been a man," Chase replied, "and there's no telling where anything alive might go."

But there was no more clue for those who searched on the rugged easterly side of the township than there had been for those who searched on the more settled westerly part.

At sundown the two groups met at the cabin. Ma stood ready to give them the food that had been simmering through the day in the big cauldron, but her smile of welcome faded when she realized that there was no man among the twenty who had anything to report.

Pa went toward her. "We're all hungry."

Bowls were filled and soon emptied; few words were spoken. As the men turned away to go to their own homes, each one went up to Ma and gave the only comfort in his power to give: "We'll be back with the light."

That night Joseph and Reuben kept watch by the fire, and Ma rested in the cabin. Only by being near Pa could she be sure that he would take the sleep he needed after his long day and before another one to follow.

The three youngest children were soon asleep; the two older boys spelled each other as they kept the fire. Ma felt restless. It was easier to bear anguish during the day when there was work to put the hands to. Darkness filled her mind with pictures of all the things that might have happened to Sarah.

Pa stood beside her and put his arms around her.

"She's so small," Ma said, sobbing against Pa's shoulder.

"Sarah is big for her years and she's got good sense."

"But—but—"

"Every man in the countryside is doing what he can to help find Sarah," Pa said in the low tone of voice that he used when he gentled an animal. "The Lord will help us all."

Ma nodded.

"We'll find her tomorrow," Pa promised.

Chapter Three
The Search Widens

Next morning the twenty men of Warren were joined by as many more, for the news was spreading over the mountains and down into the valleys. Some who came from far away rode horses that had been taken from shafts or plows. One man who came all the way from Newbury on the west side of the Connecticut River rode a white horse that had recently foaled. Beside the mare trotted the little filly, who was interested in everything, but in nothing so much as nuzzling the mother.

"We're from Wentworth," the spokesman for a group of new arrivals said.

"I'm from Romney, and my two brothers here come from Orford."

"We're from Piermont."

"The men of Haverhill have yet to find their match," a powerful man with a voice as big as his body shouted.

Pa and Uncle Chase welcomed them all and gave them directions. Samuel Richardson and Joseph Patch were designated additional leaders. Now there were four groups taking the points of the compass to penetrate the forest. Areas already searched would be searched again and communication would be constant.

"A dinner horn on Moose Hillock can be relayed to a party near the Webster Slide within minutes," Uncle Chase said. "And the first man to send the three short sharp blasts into the air will be—"

"Our man!" roared a dozen voices.

So they went off, some boastfully, some doggedly, all hopefully; but ears craving to hear the three sharp blasts went hungry. Only the low, slow sound that kept contact wailed repeatedly through the mountains during the long hours of the second day of the search.

That sunset, as they gathered before the Whitcher cabin and Ma with Mrs. Patch's help ladled food into wooden bowls, the last man in came running down from the ridge.

"Footprints!" he shouted. "I've seen footprints in the sand along Berry Brook not a mile from where we're standing."

All eyes turned on him.

"Footprints?" The word ran through the group. With some it was an exclamation, with some a question.

"A child's?" Pa asked.

The man nodded, glancing from Pa to Ma.

"Beside the child's footprints were the paw prints of a bear." He splayed his right palm and pressed it to the earth to give some indication of size.

There was silence.

"She's been torn in pieces," one of the men said.

"She's eaten up," another agreed.

Ma put her apron up to her face to catch a sob, then she drew the children closer to her. Ollie whimpered and Joseph threw his arm around him.

"If it's a she-bear," Uncle Chase said slowly, "like as not the child will be unharmed."

The meal was soon finished. Then the men turned away, but not before they had said, "We'll be back with the light."

Down the hill to their cabins went the men of Warren, while those who had come from a distance made camp in the woods and vowed they would be the first to start on the search when morning came.

"The news has got to Plymouth now," Samuel Richardson said as he mounted his horse. He had to get back as quickly as possible to chores that generally demanded a day and now must be done in a single hour of dusk.

"If the news gets to Concord and the militia come to join the search, I doubt that they'd find her even then," one of the men from Piermont murmured. But he had no intention of giving up the search.

Wednesday was a day like the other two, bright and fair; men went into it with hope, spurred on by the clue of the footprints. The area near where they had been seen was gone over and over, but nothing more came to light. The clue proved to be of no worth, but not without meaning, many of the men thought. Wednesday's end was like that of the other days as the sun set behind the mountains and the searchers returned without Sarah.

"She will never be found," they agreed among themselves as they ate the food the women had prepared for them.

Despair attached itself to weariness. They had been beaten by circumstances, and shaking their heads sadly, they were ready to admit defeat. When the time came to leave, each man in his own way told John Whitcher he would not be back.

Pa nodded as he grasped the hands of his neighbors and thanked them for the help they had given. But when Ma saw them sling their horns over their shoulders and pick up axes and guns, she ran to the ridge ahead of them and down the bridle path.

Standing in the middle of the path as they approached, she held out her hands to stop them. "Please, please," she implored, "don't leave us now."

The men stopped in their tracks and stared at her.

Ma opened her hands toward them as if to beg some kindness. "One more day, please."

Heads began to shake. *Useless . . . hopeless . . .* were the words that passed among them.

"Kind friends, strangers, whoever you may be," Ma said in the gentling tone she had learned from Pa, "for the love you bear your own little ones, help us to find our child."

They could have brushed past her as if she had been a sapling gotten across their path, but no one moved.

Ma dropped her hands and waited.

The men looked away from her and at each other. Heads began to nod; a few words were murmured among them.

"We'll be back," one of them said gruffly.

Ma stepped aside to let them pass. "God bless you," she whispered as they went by her.

After the last man had disappeared from sight, Ma sank to her knees in a crumpled heap at the base of an oak tree. She prayed then, as she had not prayed before. She prayed as she knew her husband had been praying all along, and she remembered what he had said to her: "The Lord will help us."

When she returned to the cabin, she told her husband that the men had agreed to come back the next morning.

"It's too much to ask of them," Pa replied, but there was relief in his face. "They have their own work to do, and they've given three days to us now. But one more—"

"Yes, one more, John." She slipped her hand into his as if she were sure now, then she smiled up at him.

Into the clearing came the two Richardson boys and Little John, his hand on Ollie's shoulders. Ollie, hitched to the cart, was straining to draw its load.

"Ma thought you might need something to feed the folks tomorrow," the older boy said, "and she's coming up to be with you."

"Ollie wanted to help," Little John added.

Ma looked at the load and saw a bushel basket of beans, shelled and ready to be cooked. "That will feed a mighty lot of people," she said. "I'm thankful to have so much. You tell your mother so. And tell her I'll appreciate her coming up to help."

The Richardson boys turned and raced each other down the hill while Ollie drew the cart up close to the cauldron. Then Little John freed him from the harness and put his arms around the shaggy dog to thank him for his work.

"Will we find Sarah tomorrow?" he asked.

"Yes."

"You've been saying that every day."

"I'll go on saying it."

Pa smiled at Ma, proud of her, then he tousled Little John's red hair.

"John," Ma said impulsively, "let the boys and me go along with you tomorrow."

Seeing the entreaty in his wife's face, the eagerness in his son's, Pa could not refuse. He nodded.

Little John made a glad sound, then ran off to tell his brothers.

Chapter Four
Deep in the Forest

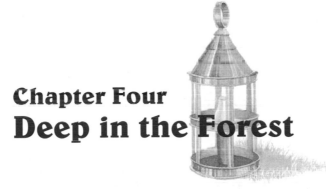

That Sunday night, when Sarah had heard the rain pattering on the leaves high above her head, she knew that she must find some kind of shelter. It was dark in the forest and everything looked different. Peering around her, she saw something in the distance that looked like a cabin. She went toward it, not running now, but walking with careful steps and listening, listening. Reaching it she saw that it was a huge rock.

"It might be a kind of cabin," she said to herself, "a cabin made of stone instead of logs."

Keeping one hand on its rough side, she walked around it slowly, looking for a door. There was none, only a hollow place under one side. She looked into it, dropped to her knees, and crawled in. She found only dry, crumpled leaves that had a queer smell, but she rested there for a while before crawling back out. Then she leaned against the rock, thinking that when Pa came with his lantern, she would show him the place that went down under the rock and ask him what it was.

"Pa!" she called again. "Ma!"

Far away there was the sound of a brook running over stones and falling in cascades. Berry Brook was near home. Pa would come for her soon.

She saw a dark shape moving among the trees and wondered what it was. She crouched down beside the boulder and stared into the darkness as the shape came toward her.

"Ollie!" she exclaimed.

It looked like Ollie, even though he seemed so much bigger than when he was back at the cabin. But then everything was different in the dim light—trees and rocks and . . .

Maybe Ollie just looked bigger, Sarah thought. Maybe she, too, would look so much bigger that Ollie wouldn't know who she was and would walk right by her.

"Ollie," she called to him, hoping he would recognize her voice.

He came nearer and made a snuffling sound.

Sarah took a few steps forward to meet him. She tried to put her arms around him and hug him because he was there and had found her. When she had to reach up to get her arms around his neck and bring his muzzle down to her face, she wondered if it really was Ollie.

He not only looked bigger, he was bigger. He had the same queer smell as the leaves she had rested on, and his coat was rough and wet. Then all doubts were swept away as a warm red tongue began licking her cheeks, licking her arms and the scratches on them.

Finding the bunch of flowers Sarah was still clutching tightly in one hand, the inquisitive nose did not pass over them. Without wasting any time, strong white teeth began to crunch the flowers. Sarah was surprised, because she had not known Ollie to eat flowers before; but she was glad she had something he liked to reward him for coming to her.

When the flowers were all gone, she held her head close to his and stroked him with both hands.

"Ollie," she whispered, "let me ride on your back when we go home."

Ollie bumped himself hard against Sarah. Puzzled, she soon realized she would have to do what he wanted her to do and that was take shelter under the rock. Nuzzling her toward the hollow place, he pushed her into it.

When Ollie followed her, there was scarcely room for them both, but Ollie soon flattened his body against the wall, lying down on his side and taking up most of the space.

"Oh, Ollie, I'm so glad we've found each other." Sarah burrowed her head against him. "But you're wet and you smell!"

Reaching around her with a front paw, Ollie swatted her gently, drawing her into the curve made by his body. She fitted into the place as she had so often when they lay together by the hearth in Pa's cabin. From the shaggy body that encircled her small one came a deep humming sound.

"Ollie Oliverian, shall I tell you how you got your name?" At home Pa would be telling stories as Ma sat by the hearth with Baby Henry on her lap and the others close by. It made Sarah feel near them if she did what they were doing.

The humming sound seemed to be Ollie's way of saying yes.

"When you were a tiny, tiny puppy, Ollie, no bigger than my hand . . ." she began. To make sure he understood, she put her hand under his chin and rubbed him. "Pa brought you home to be a help to him. As soon as we played together, Pa knew what your name would be because he said you were as roistering as the Oliverian River, so that's how . . . you got your . . . name. . . ."

The words became slow-paced, farther and farther apart, for Sarah was beginning to feel sleepy. She was so warm and comfortable, and the sound that rumbled from deep within Ollie had the same effect as when Ma sang to them after she had tucked them all into bed at the end of a day. But Ma never let them get into bed until they had said their prayers. Sarah tried to move to find a way to her knees, but Ollie's hold tightened enough to make her realize that he didn't want her to move. She decided to pray as she was.

"Keep Pa and Ma safe, and bless . . ." Sleep overtook her before she could finish.

Later that night, when the rain ceased, the life of the forest came into its own. An owl called and another answered. There was a rush of wings as a sweep was made through the trees, and a stifled cry when a small wanderer was caught in curved talons and soon devoured. A fox barked sharply, not the questing call to one of his kind, but a warning to all kinds to take cover. Distantly, then ever nearer, shouts could be heard and the blowing of horns; lanterns began to cast shadows. Voices became distinguishable as one man called and another answered.

Two men, approaching the big boulder from opposite sides, leaned against it to consult together. One stopped in mid-sentence to listen, then pointed to the hollow that went under the rock.

"Can you hear it?"

A steady drone of snoring reached their ears.

"That varmint's got himself a nice dry bed."

"I wouldn't like to be here when he wakes up."

"No more would I without my gun."

In another moment they had gone on, keeping enough space between them so each could see the glow of the other's lantern and respond to a call if it was made. After a while, silence settled over the forest. Creatures kept to their lairs and men returned to their homes.

Sarah woke and rubbed her eyes, wondering where Betsey was and why it was so quiet in the cabin; then she remembered. She was alone now, but the place where Ollie had been lying was still warm. Bending her head to look out from the shelter, she saw Ollie disappearing in the distance, walking as if he knew where he was going.

"Ollie," she called. "Ollie, wait for me."

He did not heed her voice, nor did he turn around.

Surprised at his behavior, she soon told herself that Ollie had gone to get Pa and would bring him to where she was. She would stay there until they both came back. Hunching herself down again, she looked around her to see if there was any redding-up to do as Ma did first thing in the cabin, but there was scarcely enough light yet to see by. She curled up in the warm hollow and went to sleep again.

When she wakened, daylight had found its way into the shelter. Sarah, looking around her, could see that the bed of leaves needed to have nothing done to it, and the cocoons and lichens on the rock walls and ceiling looked as if they had always been there. She crawled out and found a patch of sunlight that felt as warm as Ollie's shaggy body. Then she looked around for something to eat.

There didn't seem to be anything, and she wondered if she should go back to the clearing where she had feasted on ripe strawberries. She decided to stay near the big rock so when Ollie came back with Pa, and maybe Ma, he would find her easily. She spied a hemlock with low sweeping branches, and its tender tips of new growth offered her all she could eat for awhile. Satisfied, she sat down on the soft ground and played games with a collection of cones. When she tired of that, she built houses of twigs with clumps of moss for roofs.

In the far distance, and at different times during the day, she heard voices and dinner horns. Once she thought she heard her own name being called. Stopping her play to listen, she became quite sure that it was her name, but it wasn't Pa's voice. She stood up with her back against a tree and shouted as loud as she could, "Here I am!"

Echoing through the woods, her own voice came back to her.

She tried again. "Pa! Ma!" and then with all her strength, "Ollie!"

Only an echo answered.

It gave her a queer feeling, as if there were someone else in the woods who was trying to be Sarah. She decided not to answer anymore. The sounds of calling and horns grew more distant; then they became so faint that she lost them altogether. It must have been somebody else who was being called. Not Sarah Whitcher.

Chapter Five
Wandering Sarah

When it began to grow dusky, Sarah caught sight of Ollie. He was loping along through the trees, alone as he had been yesterday, swinging his head from side to side. She ran to meet him. Putting her face to his nose, she reached up to get her arms around his neck.

"Oh, Ollie, where's Ma and Pa? I'm so hungry."

He pushed her with his head, and when they got to the boulder, he thumped her so she tumbled in among the dry leaves. There was something odd about the way he treated her, but she was so relieved to see him that she started laughing out loud. Then when he followed her into the hollow, she pummeled him and pulled his hair, trying to find his tail.

Ollie was in no mood for a game. With one sweep of a forepaw he pulled her against his body, lay down, drew up his rear paws with his front paws tucked in close, and started licking her, vigorously, methodically.

"You're tickling me, Ollie!"

The embrace tightened, then the humming began.

Sarah's day had been long and lonely, but now that Ollie had come back to her she felt companioned.

"Shall I tell you a story, Ollie Oliverian, the way I did last night?"

The humming seemed to increase.

"Long, long ago, when Pa came to Pine Hill to build a cabin for us to live in, he sometimes got very hungry. There weren't any chickens to lay eggs for him and no cow to give him milk. If a partridge flew by, Pa might catch it to roast over his fire, or a rabbit might come along to be made into a stew, but when nothing came by do you . . . know . . . what he did?" As drowsiness began to creep over her, Sarah pushed herself deeper into her furry haven; but she wanted to finish her story. "Do you . . . know . . . he went to sleep?"

Her eyes closed. She brought her two hands together into a tight ball. She would do what Pa did when he was hungry and go to sleep.

The humming sound went on and on.

Wakened by Ollie's shift of position, Sarah saw dim light in the forest beyond the boulder. This morning she determined to follow Ollie when he crawled out into the open. She would follow him back to where Pa was instead of waiting for Pa to come to her.

As soon as Ollie shook himself out of the bed of leaves, Sarah pursued him. She had to run to keep him in sight as he loped away in the direction of the running brook. In the stillness of dawn, the sound of water made Sarah painfully aware of her thirst. She wondered if she could get to the water before her throat dried so that she would not be able to swallow. She didn't try to call his name again. It hadn't done any good. Catching up with Ollie at the brook, she waited for him to have his fill.

When he finished, he shook his head from side to side in a way she had never seen him do at the cabin, but she took it as answer to her earnest plea to wait for her before he went to Pa. She approached the sandy place and, kneeling a little upstream, put her face to the water. She drank and drank, then took time to wash her face and hands. When she stood up, Ollie was not waiting for her. He had gone away without her. She tried to find his tracks, but lost them in the underbrush, so she decided to return to the brook and wait for him there.

"Please come back soon, Ollie," she said aloud. There was not much likelihood of his hearing her, she knew, but the sound of her own voice was a change from the quietness around her. "And bring Ma and Pa with you."

Moving away from the sandy place to where the brook slipped over flat stones, she squatted down and started to build a dam. If her brothers had been there, Reuben would soon have found a way to make a mill wheel for the water to turn.

"Bring Joseph and Reuben and Little John back with you, Ollie," she called.

When she had finished her dam, she was pleased with the small contained pool of water that made a washing place.

"And, Ollie, you might as well bring Betsey and Baby Henry, for here is a good place for her to wash his things."

When hunger began to ache inside Sarah, she stopped playing and looked for something to eat. Cress was growing in the brook. She pulled some. It tasted good. She pulled up handfuls and ate it, but the empty feeling soon came back again.

Watching a bird approach the brook to drink, her eyes followed its motions as it wove among bordering grasses and disappeared from sight.

She followed it to where the grasses had stilled, then pushed them aside to see better.

At that moment the ground-nesting bird flew away with a chirping sound.

Sarah looked down and saw five speckled eggs in a small, neat nest. She reached down and touched them. They were real, as real as any she had ever found for Pa in the barn, and they were warm. She put one up to her mouth, broke the shell against her teeth, and tipped her head back to let the contents run down her throat. One by one she ate them all, and the hunger pain inside her went away.

She spent the whole day in her search for more food, and by the time Ollie found her at twilight, she was no longer hungry. She was glad to see him and filled with desire for a rough-and-tumble game. In the cabin, rolling on the floor together, she had often hung onto Ollie's tail; and if he minded, he never let her know. Now, in the woods, with dusk deepening around them, he acted very differently. He didn't seem to want to play the game. She crawled under him, but he swung around quickly and sat down.

Laughing, she ran around to lean against him. He promptly got up, and when she thought her hands would grasp his tail, there was his nose in her face.

It was like a game of tag and hide-and-seek all in one. The more determined Sarah was to lay hands on a particular place, the more determined Ollie became to keep that place to himself. Whirling around and laughing, Sarah finally got her fingers where Ollie's tail should be, but the next moment a great paw swatted her down, knocked her over, and Ollie stood beside her growling.

"Ollie, what's happened to your tail? I don't think you've got one anymore."

The growling continued. Using one forepaw, then the other, Ollie rolled her over and over till she rolled into a depression in the ground. Getting his muzzle under her, he tossed her up in the air as Pa did a forkful of hay. She landed on the earth beside some rocks. Her head was whirling, and her body hurt as her stomach had earlier. For the first time she had felt Ollie's nails. Dazed, she watched blood seeping from long scratches on her arms and legs.

In another moment Ollie was beside her, curving his body and drawing her into the curve, tightening his hold and moaning softly, then drawing his tongue over the scratches to clean them. She put her face into his shaggy hair and whispered to him that she would not try to play with his tail again.

"But please bring Ma and Pa back with you tomorrow, please, Ollie."

The moaning ceased, in time the humming started, and Sarah's fingers wound in and around the long, deep hair on Ollie's chest.

Sleep came too soon for any stories, and sleep was sound; for the next morning when Sarah wakened, Ollie had gone. Peering around her with blinking eyes, she could not even see him disappearing in the distance as she had other mornings.

She lay still for a long time. Ollie had left her, and since he had not yet brought Pa to her, she decided that she would have to find Pa for herself. The brook was not far away, but she did not think it looked quite like Berry Brook that ran near the cabin. It was wider and the water ran deeper. She decided to follow it, thinking that perhaps it would join the brook she knew well, and then she could follow Berry Brook home.

Sarah crawled away from the rocks and stood up slowly. She smoothed her dress, which was now very dirty and torn in several places, then she found her way to the swiftly flowing stream.

There she washed her hands and scooped up mouthfuls of water that filled her so the ache within her eased. She washed her feet and debated washing her dress. It had a queer smell to it; it smelled like Ollie. Instead of washing she looked for food and took whatever offered itself—ferns, flower heads, the lichen that Pa called "poor man's bread." Occasionally something tasted so bitter that she spat it out.

The day was warm, even in the shade along the flowing water, and she felt sleepy. Turning away from the stream, she walked back again into the woods, slowly, stumbling often, as if her bare feet had stones tied to them. She fell once, and when she picked herself up, she stared at the new tear in her dress. She fell again, over a tree stump and against a rock. She did not pick herself up for a long time, not until it was well past noon.

When she resumed her journey, she saw in the distance before her something that looked like shelter, so she started toward it. The sound of flowing water disappeared behind her, and she became more aware of the sounds in the forest that were like distant voices and the blowing of horns. She had heard them so often that they seemed to belong to the forest. Sometimes near, sometimes far away, they were the wind moving in the trees, then moving off to lose itself in the sky.

Sarah stumbled on, rubbing her eyes with hands made into fists to try to see better. When she got to her goal, the shelter turned out to be the top of a pine tree blown from its base in a recent storm. The needles were still green, and there was the strong smell given off by oozing sap. Working her way in and under the branches, she wondered if Ollie would be able to find her; but she was too tired and hungry and hurting to think beyond that first wondering.

Curling herself up with her head on her arms and her knees drawn close to her chin, she went to sleep. The sun had not yet set and the light had not yet become shadowy.

Ollie found her hours later. Lying down beside her, he curved his body to hers and began humming. Sarah opened her eyes a moment and loosed one hand to stroke him.

"Tomorrow, Ollie, please take me to Ma. Please, God," she whispered as she snuggled deeper into the warm comfort of Ollie's embrace.

Chapter Six
A Stranger with a Dream

As soon as the sun came over the mountains on Thursday, promising a fourth day of fine weather, the search was resumed. A few of the men who lived at a great distance had to return to their own duties, but their places were taken by Ma and the three Whitcher boys. No doubt was in their minds, especially in Little John's, that this was the day Sarah would be found. When they started out, Little John was dragging behind him the cart with its pine-slab wheels.

"The ground is too rough, son," Pa said. "There's brush in many places, often stumps. When we go high, there will be rocks. Much of the way there'll be no bridle path to follow."

"Could be she'll be tired and want to ride."

"It could be, and she will—on our shoulders."

"My shoulders, Pa?"

"She'll have her turn with each of us."

Little John trundled the cart over to Betsey and offered it to her for the day. She was pleased. It would make up to her for not going off with the rest of the family. Ma had put her in charge, not only of Baby Henry, but of the cabin.

"You're needed here, Betsey, and Ollie will stay by to help you."

"Yes, Ma."

Mrs. Patch and Mrs. Richardson, each one with a small child, had come to the cabin to prepare food and have all in readiness for the searchers' return. Betsey stood beside them. They watched the party go off, dividing at the ridge as they had other days, each group taking a different direction. Faint and far away grew the sound of the horns, but the sound was always in the air like a low, moaning wind.

"I'd like to be with them," Mrs. Patch said.

Mrs. Richardson agreed. "But somebody's got to keep the fire and see to the food."

Betsey tugged at Mrs. Patch's skirt. "Once upon a time I found a four-leaf clover in the pasture," she confided. "'If they'd let me go along, I could find my sister." She lifted her head. "I'm sure I could."

"Bless you, child, but it would take more than four-leaf clover eyes to find her." She put her arms around the little girl, sensing her need for comfort, then she released her with a sturdy shove. "Let's get to our work, for we've all got something to do. Betsey, fetch buckets so we can have the water we need, then take care of those children so none of them get too near the fire. That toddler of mine is apt to go most anywhere if you don't keep an eye on him."

Betsey got the buckets, then she tied Ollie to the cart, piled the two visiting children in with Baby Henry and went off to a shady place by the pasture wall. She had a fund of stories to tell and some songs to sing. When the little ones began to get restless, Ollie helped to keep them entertained. When he swung his tail, the children played with it as if it were a rope; when he lowered his body, they climbed up onto his back.

The two women sat on the bench by the cabin, fingering through the bushel of beans for bits of shell or stem. When the water in the cauldron over the fire came to a good rolling boil, they tipped the beans into it, added a large hunk of salt pork and a dozen or more onions.

"That'll be a tasty mess five hours from now," Mrs. Patch said as she watched the big brown bubbles form closely and then break away.

"There may be those without the heart to eat."

"I hope not. I'd like to think that success will be theirs today and they'll return with appetites worthy of all we've got in this cauldron."

"My man says that child couldn't have survived one night in the forest, leastways four. The days may be warm enough, but the nights can still chill the marrow in your bones. And what did she have on but a little thin cotton dress!"

Mrs. Patch made no comment.

"There isn't any one of all those men out scouring the mountains day after day who believes she'll be found. Alive, that is."

"Yes, there is." Mrs. Patch was quick in her reply. "John Whitcher."

"Well, he's her father!"

When it was almost noon, the children were summoned and fed. There was cold mush remaining from the morning meal, and plenty of milk. The aroma from the cauldron was beginning to penetrate the air, and Betsey sniffed excitedly.

"Will we be having beans, too?"

"Yes, child, there's enough to feed forty men, but they won't all want to eat hearty."

When Mrs. Richardson started to gather the children up to get them into the cabin for a rest, she included Betsey, who objected. "Ma put me in charge. I'm staying here with you."

"So she did, but you'll do better later on, when we'll be needing your help, if you have a mite of rest now. Come along. Neither one of us will move from this bench by the cabin until you're all awake again. It won't be any time after that before the men will be back."

"With Sarah."

It was not a question, so Mrs. Richardson did not answer.

Soon the children were tucked under a quilt in the big bed. Henry fit into the space beside Betsey's slight body, as he did against his mother's more ample one, so the Patch baby could have the use of the cradle. Ollie stretched out across the doorway.

"They'll be quiet for an hour or more."

"Then they'll be wanting something to eat."

"They can have a taste of the pottage."

The two women, sitting on the bench and leaning back against the rough wall of the cabin, took what rest they could. The sound of horns still echoed through the forest, and from hill to mountain, but so accustomed had they become to it that it was no longer even heard. Another sound caused Mrs. Patch to open her eyes drowsily. Nailed boots were striking on stones in the path. Was it another man come to join the search? Or one of the searchers returning with news?

A few moments later a young man came down the ridge and into the clearing. Neither woman had to look twice at him to see that he was a stranger. A leather sack over his shoulder proclaimed him to be a wayfarer.

"He may be wanting direction," Mrs. Richardson whispered.

"He's a beanpole of a man," Mrs. Patch added, "and he looks mile-worn."

They remained quiet as he came across the clearing to stand in front of them.

"I've come from Plymouth," he said. His words were weary, uttered through parched lips.

"Afoot? That's close to thirty miles."

He nodded.

"Where are you bound?"

"To find the child."

"The child!" Both women gasped.

"Give me some food and water, for I'm faint with hunger; then show me the bridle path to the north."

"You've come to find *Sarah?*" Mrs. Richardson asked.

"If that's her name."

"I hope you know these mountains."

He shook his head. "I've never been this far north before."

The two women exchanged glances, then Mrs. Richardson spoke again, and tartly. "When forty men who know these mountains as well as they know their own clearings can't find Sarah Whitcher, how is it you think you can?"

"Please, kind ladies, I've walked from Plymouth. I've not stopped for rest or food along the way. Give me something to eat."

" 'Tis a mess of beans cooking for the men's supper," Mrs. Patch said as she fetched a bowl, then ladled a generous portion into it. "This will put strength into you. Sit down now and eat."

Mrs. Richardson handed the young man a noggin of water. "It's the last day for the search."

He took it and bowed slightly to each woman. "My name is Heath," he said, "and I thank you kindly." Shifting the leather sack from his shoulders, he leaned it against the cabin, then sat down on the bench. The noggin of water was drained and refilled before he turned himself to the bowl of bean pottage.

"I doubt that they'll find Sarah now." Mrs. Richardson shook her head sadly. "Not even her little body or any tatters of her clothes; but there'll be a good meal waiting for them all when they get back."

"I shall find her," Mr. Heath said quietly.

"You!"

When he had finished, he set the bowl down on the bench, shook his head at the offer of more, and said, "Last night, when I walked into the inn at Plymouth, I heard talk of a lost child. I prayed that she would be found, and when I went to bed I dreamed of finding her."

"A dream!" Mrs. Richardson exclaimed, then she burst out laughing. "It will take more than a dream to find Sarah now."

Unperturbed by her laughter and beginning to look refreshed from rest and food, Mr. Heath went on. "It was no ordinary dream. It woke me from my sleep, not once but three times."

"And in it you saw Sarah?" Mrs. Patch asked eagerly.

"I did. She was in a shelter made by boughs, and she was guarded by a bear. It was cuffing her as if it were her mother. Her mother," he repeated.

Mrs. Richardson caught her breath. "Was she alive or dead?"

"The dream only showed her in the place where she would be found."

"Pray God that you dream true!"

"And the dream woke you three times?" Mrs. Patch wanted to return to the story.

"Yes. Each time I saw more clearly, the way a bird sees the country above which it flies." Mr. Heath made a wide sweep with one of his long arms. "I saw this cabin and the path leading to it. I saw a bridle path that went into the woods in a northerly direction.

I saw the place where boughs had fallen and under them I saw the child."

"When did you leave Plymouth?"

"It must have been near midnight," he said.

"And you followed the course of the Baker River?"

"Then you came up Berry Brook?"

"I did not know the names."

At that moment Betsey, wakened by the sound of voices, came to stand in the doorway, rubbing the sleep from her eyes.

Mr. Heath stared at her. Leaning forward, he looked more closely, then he gave a slight shake of his head.

"Was this the child you saw?" Mrs. Richardson asked.

"No, but there is a resemblance. I thought, almost—no, no," he shook his head vigorously. "The child I saw had red hair."

Betsey, wide awake now, went up to Mr. Heath. "Are you going to find my little sister?"

He nodded and bent over to tighten the laces on his boots. "If someone will put me on the bridle path to the north."

Joseph Patch came out of the woods and approached the cabin. His gun was carried in his right hand, and a dinner horn damp from much blowing hung over one shoulder.

"Husband!" his wife cried as she ran toward him. "This young man has come to find Sarah."

"No one can. Now."

"Oh, but he has had a wonderful dream. He knows where she is. He will show you."

Joseph Patch shook his head wearily.

Taking hold of his arm, she started toward the cabin with him. Her tone changed from one of joyous excitement to something more serious. "I think that you must heed him, husband."

Joseph Patch looked long and hard at the stranger on the bench by the cabin, as if in this last moment he might be willing to believe anything. "So?"

Mr. Heath rose and went up to him. "Can you show me the place where a bridle path going north crosses a good-sized brook?"

"That will be the Oliverian. We call it a river. I know the place."

Speaking slowly to give meaning to his words, Mr. Heath explained, "A few rods southeast of the crossing there is a pine top lying on the ground. Under it is where the child will be found."

"That crossing is close to an hour's walk from here."

"No matter."

Too tired to question further, too tired even to doubt, Joseph Patch nodded to his wife, then turned back to face the forest. "I'll show you where it is."

Without another word, Mr. Heath fell into step beside him, and the two men went off toward the ridge, arms swinging, long legs loose in their stride.

Chapter Seven
End of the Search

The two men said little as they walked up and over the ridge, then took the bridle path to the north. Only once did they stop. That was where the path crossed the Oliverian River. It was a shallow place, and both men knelt to drink and refresh themselves.

On the far side of the brook, Joseph Patch said, "Now you're the one to lead."

"And I will," Heath replied. Walking forward a few steps, he hesitated for a moment, then turned to the left and plunged into some low-growing brush.

"There's no way there. You'd best come back."

"It's my way, and it's the way I'm going."

Drawn by the young man's sureness and his own desire not to lose another person, Patch followed. "How far are you going in this?"

"A few rods. Bear to the southeast and hold to your bearings. Keep within sound of my voice."

Ahead of him Heath saw a massive pine, its top blown off in a recent gale, its gaping trunk open like a wound to the sky. Eagerly he thrust his way to where the blown top lay and saw the child just as he had seen her in the dream, asleep. But alone. He paused until Joseph Patch came up beside him and both stood gazing at little Sarah Whitcher, lost and now found. Her face was stained, her dress was torn, her arms and legs were scratched; but her lips were parted slightly and her chest rose and fell with her breathing.

"You be the one to wake her," Heath said quietly. "Likely she knows your face, and I'd be a stranger."

"She knows me 'most as well as any of my own little ones." Patch handed his gun to Heath. "When I have her close folded in my arms, fire. The signal is three shots in quick succession; wait till the count of five, then fire another two in rapid succession: *found alive.*"

Patch reached in through the tangle of branches where Sarah lay asleep. He put his arms under her and gently lifted her up.

Sarah opened her eyes. "I want my mother," she murmured. Putting her head against the friendly shoulder, she whispered, "Carry me home to my mother."

Heath fired the three shots, waited the required time, then fired the two that completed the story. Almost like an echo, the mountain world came alive with sound—shots were fired, dinner horns were blown, people could be heard shouting.

The two men walked back through the brush to the bridle path at the crossing of the Oliverian, and while they waited, Joseph Patch gave Sarah a drink of the clear cold water. Soon others began to gather around them, coming up the path, down the path, and out of the woods, all eager for a sight of the child.

"It's true! The little one has been found!"

"She's alive! God be praised!"

Men who had secretly disbelieved she would ever be found were hard put to understand how it had come about. They turned from her to the young man for explanation. Over and over he repeated the words, "I saw her in a dream. Mr. Patch led me to the place."

Ashamed now of his first unwillingness, Joseph Patch shook his head. "He would have found her without me. He was that sure."

When the Whitchers arrived, panting from their long run over rough ground, a shout went up from the crowd. Everyone spoke at once about the young man and his dream, pointing to him, gesturing. They fell back to make way for Ma and Pa in their midst, then Joseph Patch stepped forward to place Sarah in her mother's arms.

"Sarah! Sarah, our little Sarah!" Ma cried. Whatever words might have followed were lost in the tears of joy that overcame her.

Then Sarah saw her father and reached for him.

He swung her up in his arms and held her above his head while men cheered and the three boys danced around him shouting, "Sarah's been found! Our sister's been found!" Pa soon put her back in Ma's arms.

The stranger in the crowd was the young man standing near Joseph Patch. Pa went up to him and grasped one hand in both of his. Pa's pale blue eyes looked into the young man's, and words he might never be able to say were in his long glance. Like the dropping of a wind, silence settled through the crowd. Only the Oliverian, rushing over its rocky bed on its way to the valley, could be heard.

"I didn't know what the Lord was going to do nor how He'd do it," John Whitcher said, "but I knew He'd do something. And He did."

Silence again, and the river running through it; silence broken by a child's voice saying, "He made everything come out right."

"Amen," someone on the edge of the crowd murmured. It was repeated until everyone had said it not once but many times; repeated until it became a great rolling sound that wrapped them all up in wonder at what had happened.

Then they started down the bridle path, led by the Whitcher family.

"Want to walk." Sarah struggled in her mother's arms. "Want to walk with the people."

"Not until your brothers have had a chance to give you a ride," Pa said. He lifted her free, then set her first on Little John's shoulders. After a few rods along the path, he lifted her up again and placed her on Reuben's, and finally on Joseph's shoulders.

"Where's Ollie?"

"Waiting for you at home."

It took almost an hour to reach the cabin, but the news went ahead. The signal, heard and understood by the women, set them to speeding up preparations for the meal. When the three boys came running into the clearing with the full story, the women listened eagerly. Nothing would do for them then but to leave the boys in charge of the fire and the pottage and go up the path to see for themselves and welcome the little girl.

Mr. Heath walked behind Ma and Pa, enjoying the sight of Sarah's red head bobbing above her father's as she rode on his shoulders. She had accepted a piece of bread someone put in her hands but soon discovered that a few bites were all she wanted. Too happy to try to swallow and excited by all the attention she was getting, Sarah offered the bread to Mr. Heath, who took it from her with a word of thanks.

Everyone wanted to touch her. Everyone wanted to ask her about the time in the forest.

"Weren't you lonely?"

"Weren't you frightened?"

Over and over the same questions were asked as more searchers came out of the woods and caught up with the crowd going down the path. To them all Sarah had the same answer. "Ollie came to me every night and kept me warm."

When she first said it, Pa had looked sharply at Ma. Ollie spent the nights outside to guard the stock, but had he gone to the forest to be with Sarah, he would have brought her home as he sometimes did a lamb or a calf that had strayed. Ma knew what Pa meant.

Now, perched on Pa's broad shoulders, Sarah began to sing to herself about her shaggy dog, her big black dog whose name was Ollie Oliverian and whose coat was warmer than any blanket.

When they got within sight of the cabin, she spied Ollie in the doorway with Betsey beside him, and she begged Pa to put her down. Standing unsteadily for a moment, then tottering as she ran, Sarah went toward the cabin calling Ollie's name.

He didn't move except to wag his tail uncertainly.

Just before Sarah reached him, she stopped short. "You've grown so small, Ollie! What's happened to you?"

He took a step toward her, then halted. Ears laid back, he stretched his neck out until his nose nearly touched her, sniffing, sniffing. His hackles rose. A low growl vibrated in his throat.

Sarah moved quickly and threw her arms around him, longing for nothing so much as to curl up against his warm body. "Sing to me, Ollie, the way you used to sing to me in the woods."

Pa and Ma drew near. Ollie looked up at them with questioning. His tail was poised, his ears were laid back, his whole attention was diverted by the strong musk smell that had always meant just one thing to him.

"Take care of her, Ollie," Pa said.

Ollie crumpled to the earth, and Sarah fitted herself against his body.

"Let her rest," Ma said. "It'll be time enough to wash and dress her when we've all had something to eat."

"She's tired from the excitement," Mrs. Patch agreed, while Mrs. Richardson stared at the little girl as if she could not see enough of her.

The young man went toward the bench to pick up his leather sack. He slung it over his shoulder and started to make his way through the crowd that had gathered around the fire.

"You'll stay, won't you, Mr. Heath, and have some food with us?" Ma's voice was as cheerful as birdsong.

"Thank you, ma'am, but I've already had a good share. I'd best be going on my way." He smiled at her, then turned to Pa.

The two men clasped hands again.

Ma and Pa watched him as he went up to the ridge. At the top he turned and waved to them. They raised their hands and waved to him before he went from their sight.

Mrs. Patch and Mrs. Richardson had been filling bowls from the cauldron, but before anyone dipped a spoon into the pottage, there was a blessing to be said, and they waited for Pa to say it. He led them in singing "Old Hundred."

"Praise God from whom all blessings flow;
Praise Him all creatures here below—"

Men, women, children sang as they had never sung before, and Pa's voice soared above them all.

As young Mr. Heath went down the bridle path, the sound of singing went with him.

Author's Note

Is it true? That is what I asked myself when I first read the story of Sarah Whitcher in a book of New Hampshire folk tales. It must be true, I thought, some years later when I read it again in *The History of Warren, New Hampshire,* written by William Little and published in 1870. Chapter Seven bore the title: HOW SARAH WHITCHER WAS LOST IN THE WOODS; WHAT HAPPENED AND HOW THEY HUNTED FOR HER, TOGETHER WITH A REMARK- ABLE DREAM, AND HOW A BUSHEL OF BEANS DISAPPEARED.

Three strands made the story, and each one was strong: the fearlessness and resourcefulness of a lost little girl; the stalwart faith of her father, who said, "Trust in the Lord" and so held out a lifeline to all who joined in the search; and the obedience to a dream that came to a stranger, Mr. Heath. It was a story that asked to be retold for children today. So I read many books of the period, talked with Warren men and women who were descendants of the early settlers, and wrote it, keeping true to the known facts and adding only such description and conversation as was in keeping with the time.

An answer to the question that had first stirred me came one day a few months after the book was published and had begun to find its way to readers. My telephone rang. "Am I speaking to Elizabeth Yates?" a gentle voice inquired.

"Yes, you are."

"This is Alice Westneat, and I am Sarah Whitcher's great-granddaughter."

I gasped as the past seemed to overtake the present.

"I've just read your book, and I want you to know that you have told the story as we heard it as children, just as we've gone on telling it to our children and grandchildren."

Alice Westneat and I soon became friends, and she told me more about Sarah, or Sally as she was always called in the family. The little girl grew up and married Richardson French, a farmer. They had eleven children, and Sarah lived to be seventy-nine.

During the years I have signed many books for their descendants, and the last one was for Tommy and Jesse Merrill, Sarah Whitcher French's great-great-great-great grandsons.

A story such as this is part of the heritage of our pioneer past and belongs to us all, especially to children and to those who believe in miracles.

Elizabeth Yates